This Bridge

This bridge will only take you halfway there
To those mysterious lands you long to see:
Through gypsy camps and swirling Arab fairs
And moonlit woods where unicorns run free.
So come and walk awhile with me and share
The twisting trails and wondrous worlds I've known.
But this bridge will only take you halfway there —
The last few steps you'll have to take alone.

Shel Silverstein

Little People™ Big Book

About

MAGICAL WORLDS

TIME
LIFE *for*
Children™
ALEXANDRIA, VIRGINIA

Table of Contents

Once Upon a Time...
Magical Creatures Roamed Free

Once Upon a Time...
In an Enchanted Land

Once Upon a Time . . .
The Silliest Things Could Happen

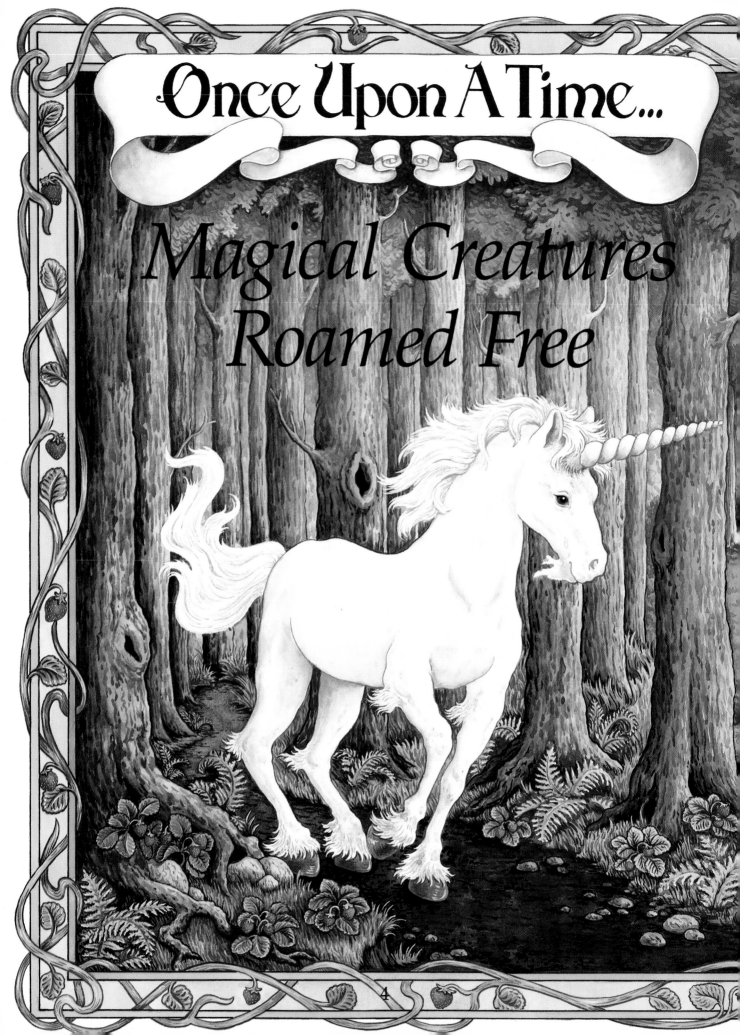

Once Upon A Time...

Magical Creatures Roamed Free

Unicorn

The Unicorn with the long white horn
  Is beautiful and wild.
He gallops across the forest green
So quickly that he's seldom seen
Where Peacocks their blue feathers preen
  And strawberries grow wild.
He flees the hunter and the hounds,
Upon black earth his white hoof pounds,
Over cold mountain streams he bounds
  And comes to a meadow mild;
There, when he kneels to take his nap,
He lays his head in a lady's lap
  As gently as a child.

William Jay Smith

Stan Bolovan and the Dragon

A Retelling of the Traditional Fairy Tale

Once upon a time, a man named Stan Bolovan and his wife lived in a small cottage deep in a forest. They had a simple but good life. Their only sadness was that they had no children.

One day Stan met a magician on the road. The magician saw that Stan was a good man, and offered to grant him one wish.

Stan knew what to ask for right away. "Please give us children!" he said. "As many as my wife wants."

"You have your wish," said the magician.

Stan rushed home. When he arrived at his house, the door opened wide, and lots and lots of children came running out. His wife followed, carrying even more children. She was bouncing with joy.

"How many do we have?" he asked.

"We now have what I've always wished for—one hundred perfect children!"

Stan loved his new children, but there was just one problem: they were eating him out of house and home! So the next morning, Stan set out to find a way to feed all those children. He took along a sack with a small lump of cheese, in case he grew hungry. He

soon found a shepherd with flocks of sheep and goats. "What can I do to earn some of your sheep?" he asked.

"Only one thing," replied the shepherd. "You must chase away the dragon who comes here every evening to steal my sheep and goats."

"I'll do it," said Stan.

Stan waited for the dragon to appear. Early that evening, when the dragon came to steal a goat, Stan confronted him. "I am Stan Bolovan," he shouted. "I'm here to protect these sheep and goats. Stay away from here!"

"Just try and stop me, you fool!" roared the dragon.

"Why, I can destroy you just by looking at you!" said Stan. He reached into his sack and pulled out his cheese. "Go and get a stone like this one. Then try to squeeze your stone so hard that buttermilk runs out of it."

The dragon fetched a stone and squeezed it so hard that it turned to powder. But no buttermilk came out of it.

"You certainly are feeble," said Stan. "Now watch me!" Stan squeezed the cheese until buttermilk ran through his fingers.

This scared the dragon terribly. He thought that Stan was the strongest man he had ever seen! The dragon was not very smart, despite his great size and power.

"My mother would be happy to have someone as strong as you to work for her," said the dragon with a sneaky smile. "She'll gladly pay you

seven bags of gold for each day you work."

"I could use the money," said Stan. "I've got a hundred children to feed, you know."

So Stan and the dragon set off down the road together. After walking along a narrow, bushy path, they came to the cave of the dragon's mother.

"Mother, you must get rid of this

man!" whispered the dragon to his mother. "He is strong and dangerous!"

"He won't be a problem for *me*," replied the dragon's mother, turning around to get a good look at Stan. He didn't look so very strong to *her*.

"Show us how strong you are," she said to Stan, pointing to a huge club. "My son will throw this club. See if you can throw it farther than he can."

The dragon picked up the gigantic club as if it were a twig and sent it flying over the trees for at least five miles. Stan, the dragon, and the dragon's mother chased after it. By the time they found the club, the moon was high in the sky. Stan

leaned down and tried to lift the club off the ground. It was terribly heavy. He had barely lifted it when he set it back down again.

"What are you doing?" asked the dragon.

"Waiting for the moon to get out of the way," explained Stan. "If I throw the club now, it will surely hit the moon and we'll never get it back."

"But that's my favorite club!" said the dragon. "Please don't throw it! I will give you seven sacks of gold just to let me take it back."

"As you wish," said Stan. When they got back to the cave, he asked, "What's next?"

"Let's see who can bring the most water back here before the sun rises," said the dragon's mother.

The dragon ran off and soon returned with twelve buffalo skins full of water. Stan couldn't even lift a single empty skin. So he went out to the stream, sat down, and started to dig a hole. The dragon was watching closely.

"What are you doing?" asked the dragon, a little nervously.

"Well," said Stan. "I'm going to bring the whole stream into the cave. It will take only a moment."

"NO!" shouted the dragon. "I'll give you seven more bags of gold. Just

don't flood our cave!"

"As you wish," said Stan, adding the gold to his stash.

Later, everyone got ready for bed. Stan was glad, because it had been a long day and he was very tired. But he did not trust the dragons. So he stayed awake a little longer.

"Oh, me! Oh, my!" wailed the dragon to his mother. "How can we rid ourselves of this man? Soon he will have all our gold!"

"I have an idea," replied his mother. "Tonight you must sneak into his room and knock him on the head with your club. Then he'll never bother us again!"

Stan, who overheard the dragon's mother, filled a blanket with feathers and put it in his bed. Then he slid underneath the bed and began to snore loudly.

The dragon soon tiptoed into the room, as quietly as a dragon ever could. He swung his club down on the place where Stan's head should have been. Then he crept out of the room, giggling wickedly.

Then next morning, Stan strolled out to breakfast. "Look at my forehead!" he said. "A flea must have bitten me!" The dragon and his mother were very frightened. A club on the head was nothing more than a fleabite to Stan! What kind of man could he be? They heaped upon Stan all the sacks of gold they had, just to get rid of him.

Stan was glad to have all that gold, but it was far too heavy for him to carry. He knew what to do. "I'll leave on one condition," he said to the dragon, "that you carry all the gold sacks home for me. I would be ashamed to bring home so little gold myself."

"Anything you want! Anything!" cried the dragon.

Through the forest they went, and at last Stan saw his little house and heard the children's voices. Stan told the dragon, "I have one hundred children, all as strong as I am. They'll be so happy to meet you."

Suddenly the door of the house burst open, and all the children, who were very, very hungry, ran toward the dragon waving knives and forks.

"A dragon!" shouted the children. "We're going to have roast dragon for dinner!"

The dragon took one look at the hungry children, dropped the sacks of gold, and fled for his life. Stan, his wife, and their hundred children never saw that dragon again. And, thanks to the gold, they lived in comfort with plenty to eat for the rest of their days.

LITTLE RIDDLES ABOUT
BIG GIANTS

What is three stories tall, green,
and tastes good on bread?

The Jelly Green Giant!

What kind of giants can jump
higher than a house?

All kinds of giants. Houses can't jump!

What time is it when
a 500-pound giant
sits on your chair?

**Time to get
a new chair!**

How do you talk
to a 20-foot-tall giant?

Use BIG words!

Why did the giant
wear red suspenders?

To keep his pants up!

Where do giants sleep?

Anywhere they want to!

13

Thumbelina

A Retelling of the Fairy Tale by Hans Christian Andersen

nce upon a time, a woman wished upon a flower bud for a child. To her surprise, the flower burst open, and in the soft, delicate center sat a teeny, tiny girl. "Why, you're no bigger than my thumb," said the woman. "I think I'll call you Thumbelina."

The woman set up a little home for Thumbelina on her kitchen table. During the day, Thumbelina sang for the woman in a voice as sweet as honey. Swallows from the garden chirped merrily as her chorus. At night, she slept in a polished walnut shell under a smooth rose petal.

One night, a toad hopped through an open window. "Crooaakk! How pretty she is!" she said when she saw Thumbelina. "She'll make a fine wife for my son." And with that, the toad lifted the walnut shell, which was as light as a feather, and carried it away to the brook where she lived with her son.

"Brek-a-brek-brek," said the son when he saw Thumbelina.

"Shhh," said his mother. "You'll wake her. We mustn't let her escape. You shall marry her in the morning." Before going to bed, the two toads swam to a water lily and put the walnut cradle on one of its leaves.

During the night, a strong gust of wind came. Trees swayed, the water in the brook rippled, and the leaf that held Thumbelina's cradle broke away from the water lily. The leaf carrying poor little Thumbelina began to drift downstream.

When Thumbelina woke up, she didn't know where she was. At first she was frightened, but once she saw the beautiful flowers on the riverbank, she felt very happy—so happy she began to sing. And it wasn't long before buzzing bees, singing birds, and chirping crickets all chimed in. It was like an orchestra!

Thumbelina soon grew hungry. As she watched a pretty butterfly, she had an idea. She untied her hair ribbon and tied one end to the butterfly and the other end to the leaf. The butterfly flew toward shore, pulling the leaf and Thumbelina along with it. Thumbelina stepped off the leaf onto land and thanked the butterfly for helping her. Then she climbed into the prettiest wildflower and drank its delicious honey. When twilight came, Thumbelina wove a tiny hammock from blades of grass,

hung it between two daisies, and
went to sleep.

For the rest of the summer,
Thumbelina happily lived alone.
Every morning, she ate honey from
flowers and drank morning dew from
the leaves. And every night, she slept
in her tiny hammock.

Autumm came, and the air became
cold, leaves fell off the trees, and
birds began to fly south. But worst
of all, the flowers wilted, leaving no
honey for Thumbelina. Then one
day it snowed. Poor Thumbelina! One
snowflake was the size of her hand!
Shivering, Thumbelina went in search
of food and warmth.

It wasn't long before she stumbled

upon the hole of a field mouse. "Come
in," said the field mouse. "You're
just in time for dinner!" Thumbelina
and the field mouse had a delicious
meal of corn and hot cider. After
dinner, Thumbelina told stories and
sang. The field mouse enjoyed it so
much, she asked Thumbelina to stay.

One day, the field mouse's next-
door neighbor, a mole, came to visit.
The mole wore a thick, black, velvety
coat and lived in a home that was
twenty times the size of the field
mouse's. The mouse, who was very
fond of the mole, listened closely as
he talked for hours about all his
riches. Thumbelina found the mole
to be rather boring and thought it

dreadful that he preferred his dark home underground to the sunlit sky. She listened, though, to be polite.

"Sing for us, Thumbelina," said the field mouse when the mole grew tired. When the mole heard Thumbelina's sweet, musical voice, he fell in love with her. And the next day, he dug a passageway between the two homes so he could see Thumbelina every day.

The passageway was damp and dark, and the only time Thumbelina went down there was to sweep it clean. One day when she was sweeping, she came across a swallow lying on the passageway floor. It looked as if it had frozen to death with the winter cold. She felt very

sorry for the bird and covered it with bits of leaves and hay, remembering how she used to sing with the swallows in the woman's garden. Thumbelina kissed the poor swallow's forehead, and he opened his eyes. The swallow wasn't dead, after all!

For the rest of the winter, Thumbelina nursed the swallow, giving him water from a leaf and bits of corn. Spring finally came, and the swallow had his strength back and was ready to leave. "Fly away with me," begged the swallow.

"I can't leave the field mouse. She's grown used to having me around," Thumbelina said sadly. "Good-bye, swallow!"

"Thank you for saving my life, my tiny friend," said the swallow. And he flew away.

Thumbelina went inside where the field mouse was busy sewing. "This will be your wedding gown," said the field mouse. "The mole wants you to be his wife!"

"I won't marry the mole!" said Thumbelina, horrified. "I can't live in his dark, stuffy home with no sunlight."

"Nonsense," said the field mouse. "It isn't everyday that a mole with such a great fortune should ask for your hand in marriage." There was no use arguing—the field mouse was quite stubborn. And if it hadn't been

for the field mouse, Thumbelina might not have made it through the winter. So, sadly, she prepared to marry the mole.

On the day of her wedding, Thumbelina was allowed to go outside to say good-bye to the sun. With tears in her eyes, she wished upon a flower that she wouldn't have to marry the mole.

"Tweet-tweet," sang a voice, interrupting her wish. Thumbelina looked up, and there was her friend the swallow! Thumbelina was very happy to see him and told him how she didn't want to marry the mole.

"Come with me to the warm countries where lovely flowers grow

all year around," said the swallow. And this time, Thumbelina climbed up on his soft wing and held on tightly as they soared up into the blue sky—away from the field mouse and the mole. They passed over forests, seas, mountains, and fields with magnificent flowers. The view down below was breathtaking!

At last they arrived in the warm countries, where the air smelled sweet as honey. Butterflies danced among brightly colored flowers. The swallow set Thumbelina upon a silver flower. There, in its center, stood a little man—as tiny as Thumbelina herself! He was King of the Flowers, and wore a tiny golden crown and a bright set of wings. The king thought Thumbelina was the prettiest girl in the land, and he fell in love with her. Thumbelina thought the king was very handsome, and when he said, "Will you marry me and be Queen of the Flowers?" she said yes.

The swallow sang their wedding song, and afterward, there was a delightful festival. Tiny people from all the flowers in the land came with gifts—the best gift being a set of silver wings that let Queen Thumbelina fly from flower to flower whenever she liked. And from that day on, the King and Queen of the Flowers lived together happily ever after.

Little John Bottlejohn

Little John Bottlejohn lived on the hill,
    And a blithe little man was he.
And he won the heart of a pretty mermaid
    Who lived in the deep blue sea.
And every evening she used to sit
    And sing on the rocks by the sea,
"Oh! little John Bottlejohn, pretty John Bottlejohn,
    Won't you come out to me?"

Little John Bottlejohn heard her song,
    And he opened his little door.
And he hopped and he skipped, and he skipped and he hopped,
    Until he came down to the shore.
And there on the rocks sat the little mermaid,
    And still she was singing so free,
"Oh! little John Bottlejohn, pretty John Bottlejohn,
    Won't you come out to me?"

Little John Bottlejohn made a bow,
  And the mermaid, she made one too;
And she said, "Oh! I never saw anyone half
  So perfectly sweet as you!
In my lovely home 'neath the ocean foam,
  How happy we both might be!
Oh! little John Bottlejohn, pretty John Bottlejohn,
  Won't you come down with me?"

Little John Bottlejohn said, "Oh yes!
  I'll willingly go with you.
And I never shall quail at the sight of your tail,
  For perhaps I may grow one too."
So he took her hand, and he left the land,
  And plunged in the foaming main.
And little John Bottlejohn, pretty John Bottlejohn,
  Never was seen again.

Laura Richards

The Elves and the Shoemaker

A Retelling of the Classic Fairy Tale

nce upon a time, there lived an old shoemaker and his wife. They worked hard, but never had much money, and one cold winter day they found they couldn't afford food or firewood.

What were they to do? The shoemaker needed leather to make shoes, but his leather had run out. There was only a tiny scrap left. They had no money for more.

They worried as they went to bed that night. They were sure that in the morning they would have to turn themselves out into the cold. But when they got out of bed the next morning, they found a surprise. Sitting on the cobbler's bench was a fine little pair of shoes, which had been made out of the last scrap of leather in the shop!

The shoemaker and his wife danced for joy. They held the shoes up for a closer look. Such fine, even stitches! Such a pretty style! Whoever could have done such a delicate job? While they wondered, the bell on their shop door tinkled merrily, and in came a wealthy gentleman who had seen the

shoes through the window.

The shoes were the perfect size for his youngest daughter. The gentleman gave them a gold piece for the shoes then and there. The shoemaker and his wife could hardly believe their good luck! They rushed to the market to buy enough leather to make two more pairs of shoes, and they bought some cheese and potatoes as well. Then they had their

you would have thought only mice could have made such tiny stitches.

Suddenly, the shop door opened, and in came the gentleman from the day before. His youngest daughter had loved her shoes, so the gentleman had come back to buy some for his son and his wife. He set down two gold coins and carried the new shoes away.

This was the beginning of a good

first good meal in weeks, and fell asleep content. The shoemaker was eager to begin making two new pairs of shoes in the morning.

But the morning came with another surprise. On the counter sat two pairs of shoes, made as prettily as the first pair. One had leather bows, and the other had straps and buckles. Each one had stitches as fine and small as the shoemaker had ever seen;

time for the old shoemaker and his wife. Now they could buy wood for the stove and the fireplace, thick wool scarves, and enough hot food to keep them warm, full, and cozy. Every day the shoemaker and his wife would buy more leather—and laces and buttons and bows—and leave them on the counter at night before going to bed. Every morning they found beautiful new shoes, which would be sold by noon.

Finally one evening, the wife said to her husband, "We must find out who is being so kind to us. Let us stay awake and hide behind the curtain tonight, and see who is making our shoes for us." The shoemaker agreed, and they stayed awake.

At the stroke of midnight, the door of the shop opened and in dashed two little elves dressed in rags. Without a word, they jumped upon the counter. They quickly set to work, quietly singing and laughing all the while. They were done in an hour,

leaving ten beautiful pairs of shoes behind.

The wife felt sorry for the elves. "The poor little things! Dressed only in rags! And it is so cold out! I shall make them two little suits of clothing to keep them warm."

So the wife made the elves some fine clothes. The shoemaker helped her. In a couple of days, the suits were ready. They made pants and socks, shirts and jackets, and little caps with a sparrow's feather tucked in each brim. And they finished off the outfits with two tiny pairs of shoes.

Again the shoemaker and his wife hid behind the curtain. Again at midnight the little elves came in. But this time, when they saw the fine new clothes waiting for them, they threw back their heads and laughed for joy. They dressed themselves quickly, and danced before the mirror. They then raced out the door into the icy cold, laughing and daring the wind to blow its hardest: now they would be warm forever!

The elves never came back. But by now the shoemaker and his wife had lots of happy customers who bought a great number of shoes, so the old man and his wife were never hungry or cold again.

THE FANTASTICAL FOREST

There are places to hide
And places to play
In this magical forest
So far away.

Can you find:

Two dragons in their cave?
A winged horse flying among the clouds?
Three elves hiding their gold?
A troll hiding under a bridge?
Four fairies dancing among the trees?
A tired giant?
Five unicorns playing hide-and-seek?

27

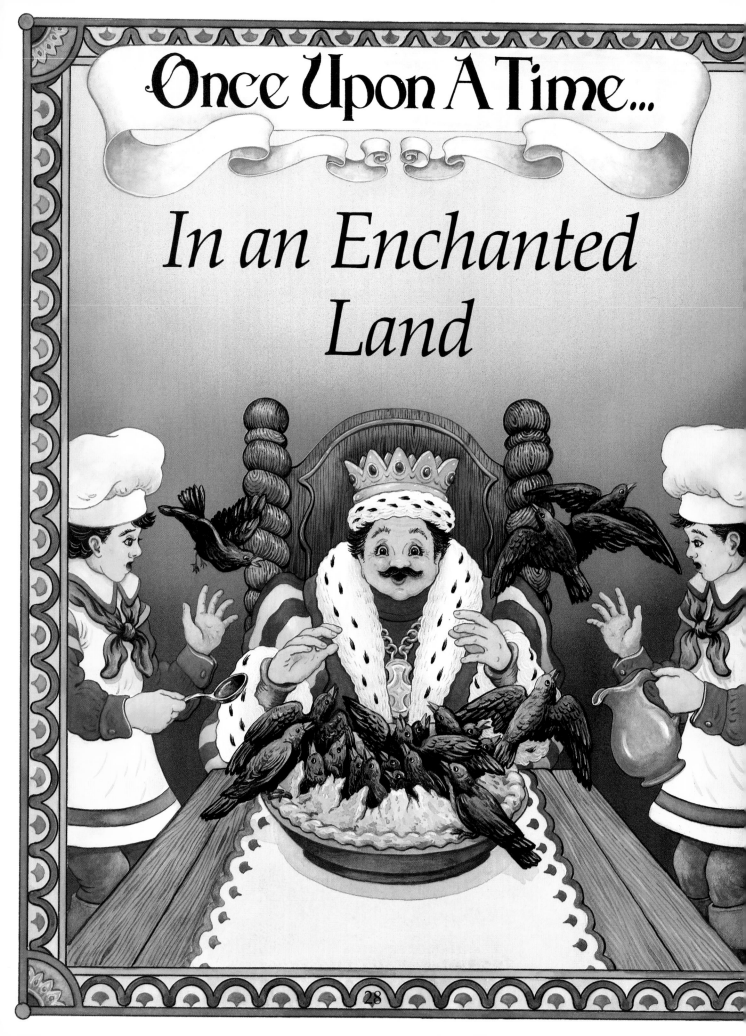

Sing a Song of Sixpence

Sing a song of sixpence,
    A pocket full of rye;
Four and twenty blackbirds
    Baked in a pie.

When the pie was opened,
    The birds began to sing;
Was not that a dainty dish
    To set before a king?

The King was in the counting house,
    Counting out his money;
The Queen was in the parlor
    Eating bread and honey.

The maid was in the garden,
    Hanging out the clothes,
When along came a blackbird
    And snipped off her nose!

Traditional

Cinderella

A Retelling of the Traditional Fairy Tale

Once upon a time, a man and his daughter lived all alone in a great big house. The mother had died some time before, and the daughter was very lonely. So the father decided to marry again to give his daughter a new mother.

The day came when the father brought his new wife home. She had two daughters of her own, and they didn't like their new stepsister. She was pretty and had a good heart, and this made them jealous. So they made her do all the cooking and cleaning, they took away all her pretty clothes, and they made her sleep in the attic. Sometimes she got so cold that she would sleep on the kitchen floor next to the fireplace, and during the night she would get covered with cinders. That is how she came to be called Cinderella.

One bright spring day, while Cinderella was working in the garden, a messenger arrived with invitations to a grand ball at the palace. All the maidens of the land were being invited. The Prince would be at the ball, where he could meet them and perhaps find a bride.

The nasty stepsisters couldn't wait for the ball. When the night finally came, they began to order Cinderella around more than ever. "Cinderella, iron my ball gown!" "Cinderella, fix my hair!" Poor Cinderella worked faster and faster, trying to get everything finished.

"Please, Stepmother, may I go to the ball, too?" asked Cinderella. "I've finished all my work, and I've helped my stepsisters get ready for the ball."

"Certainly *not!*" said her stepmother. "Look at you! You're all dirty, and

"I'm your fairy godmother! Why are you so sad?" asked the kindly woman.

"I *so* wanted to go to the ball," cried Cinderella.

"And you shall," said her fairy godmother, as she led Cinderella into the garden. The fairy godmother pointed her wand at a fat pumpkin, and instantly it became a shiny golden coach. She then touched her wand to six tiny mice, and they suddenly turned into prancing white horses. Four lizards became footmen dressed in velvet. "Now you can go to the ball!" said the fairy godmother.

you have nothing but rags to wear. How could you go to the ball like *that?*" The stepmother quickly whisked her daughters into their coach, and away they went to the palace.

Cinderella sat by the kitchen fireplace and began to cry. But suddenly a little old woman magically appeared before her. "Who are you?" asked a very surprised Cinderella.

31

"But my clothes . . . they're rags . . ."
said Cinderella. The fairy godmother
pointed her wand one last time.
Cinderella was suddenly wearing a
beautiful dress covered with sparkling
jewels. "Thank you! Oh, thank you!"
she cried.

Just before Cinderella climbed into
the coach, her fairy godmother told
her to be home before midnight, since
that was when the magic spell would
be broken. The footmen helped her
into the coach, and Cinderella was off
to the ball!

When Cinderella arrived, the
Prince couldn't take his eyes off her.
The two of them danced together
all night, and he refused to dance
with anyone else. But as midnight

approached, Cinderella said good
night and rushed away before the
Prince could even ask her name.
When the stepsisters came home,
they found Cinderella asleep next to
the kitchen fireplace, dressed in rags
as always.

The following day, it was announced
that another ball would be given that
very night. The Prince wanted to find
the mysterious, beautiful woman who
had left so quickly the night before.

The stepsisters again made Cinderella help them get ready for the ball, and again they left her behind. But this time, Cinderella's fairy godmother gave her a dress even more beautiful and more grand than the one before, and on her feet were glass slippers.

At the ball, the Prince never left her side, and Cinderella was having so much fun that she forgot about the time. Then she heard the clock begin to strike twelve. She rushed away, but as she raced down the palace steps, she lost one of her glass slippers. The Prince found it and picked it up carefully.

The next morning, the Prince vowed to marry the owner of the glass slipper. With the help of some of the King's ministers, he began to visit every household in the kingdom. Young maidens were only too happy to try on the glass slipper, but it didn't fit anyone.

Finally, the Prince came to Cinderella's house. The older stepsister's heel was too big for the slipper, and the younger sister's toes were too fat. The Prince was about to give up when he saw Cinderella working in the garden. He asked to see her.

"The slipper couldn't *possibly* fit *her*," snapped the stepmother. "It *must* belong to one of my own daughters!"

But Cinderella was brought in anyway, and she tried on the slipper. When it fit perfectly, the Prince knew he had found his true love. While the stepmother and her daughters looked on in surprise, the Prince swept Cinderella up onto his horse and took her to the palace, where she was dressed in the fine clothes of a princess.

The Prince and Cinderella were married, and lived happily ever after.

Queen Anne's Castle

Deep inside a shady wood
The Castle of Queen Anne the Good
Awaits some visitors for a feast;
They're serving roasted wildebeest!

In the Great Hall trumpets blare,
While in the kitchen cooks prepare
The silver dishes polished bright
To serve at Queen Anne's feast tonight!

The tailor sews,
The fiddler bows,
The minstrel strums,
The juggler hums,
A jangly jester takes his chance
To join a princess in a dance.

Sabers clash
While horses dash,
Armor clangs,
An arrow twangs,
Each rider tries with all his might
To prove himself the bravest knight.

A falcon soars,
The fire roars,
A church bell rings,
The choir sings,
An old wizard makes gold from stone,
And Good Queen Anne sits on her throne.

Emily James

39

Puss in Boots

A Retelling of the Traditional Fairy Tale

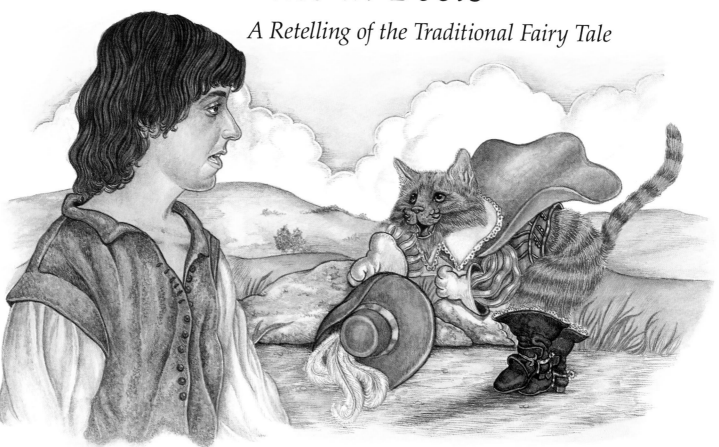

nce upon a time, in a far-off country, there lived an old miller with his son and his cat. A day came when the miller fell ill, and he said to his son, "When I die, there'll be no money for you; all you'll have to eat is the cat. You'll then have to find your way in the world as best you can."

The old father soon died, and the young man cried for him. But when he reached to grab the cat, the cat jumped away and said, "My word! You must not eat me, for I can help you find great riches."

The young man was startled, for he'd never heard the cat say so much as a "Good morning!" before. But when the cat asked for a pair of boots, the young man found a pair, and the cat looked quite charming when he stood up in them and bowed politely.

The cat scampered away, using his boots to jump more quickly than ever, and in a flash he caught a rabbit in the meadow. He took the rabbit in a sack to the King, who was hunting nearby, and said with an elegant bow, "Your Majesty, accept this rabbit as a gift from my master, the Marquis of Carabas."

Now the King had never heard of the Marquis of Carabas before. Nor had anyone else, for Puss had just

40

invented the name. But the King liked the rabbit, so he took it and told the cat to thank the Marquis of Carabas.

A little later in the day, Puss caught a quail, and again brought it to the King as a present from the Marquis. He then caught a lobster, then a trout. The King was very grateful each time, and ate very well all day long.

At the end of the afternoon, when the King was getting ready to return to his palace, Puss told his young master to take off all his clothes and jump into the lake, and to scream and shout as if he were drowning. This the young man did, with lots of splashing. The cat stood upon the bank as the King's coach went by and shouted, "Help! Thieves snatched my master, the Marquis of Carabas! They stole his royal clothes, and tossed him into the lake to drown!"

The King remembered the fine food the cat had brought him, so he stopped the carriage and ordered his men to pull the Marquis of Carabas to safety. Then he gave his own royal cloak to the young man, and sent on ahead for new clothes suitable for such a fine gentleman. Before long the young man was dried off and dressed in silks and satins, impressing the King no end. He impressed the King's daughter, too, who noticed he was quite nice.

Meanwhile, Puss had pranced on ahead. When he came to a field of workers, he told them, "If the King asks you who owns this field, you must tell him THE MARQUIS OF CARABAS." This is indeed what happened as the King's coach went rolling by, with the King's daughter and the miller's son inside it.

The cat came to a lake. "You must tell the King that THE MARQUIS OF CARABAS owns all these boats," said the cat to the fishermen, and this

42

is indeed what they said. The King was impressed, and the King's daughter thought the young man was very handsome.

The cat ran past a forest. To the hunters walking by the side of the road he said, "You must tell the King that THE MARQUIS OF CARABAS owns all these woods." So said the hunters when the King's carriage passed. The King nodded with his eyebrows raised high, and the King's daughter looked at the young man affectionately.

The cat then came to a huge castle owned by a terrible ogre. The cat stomped right in with his boots. The ogre heard the noise and came growling out of the kitchen. "Who dares to enter my castle?" the ogre spat.

"Only I, little Puss," said the cat. "The workers in the fields say you have magic powers and can turn

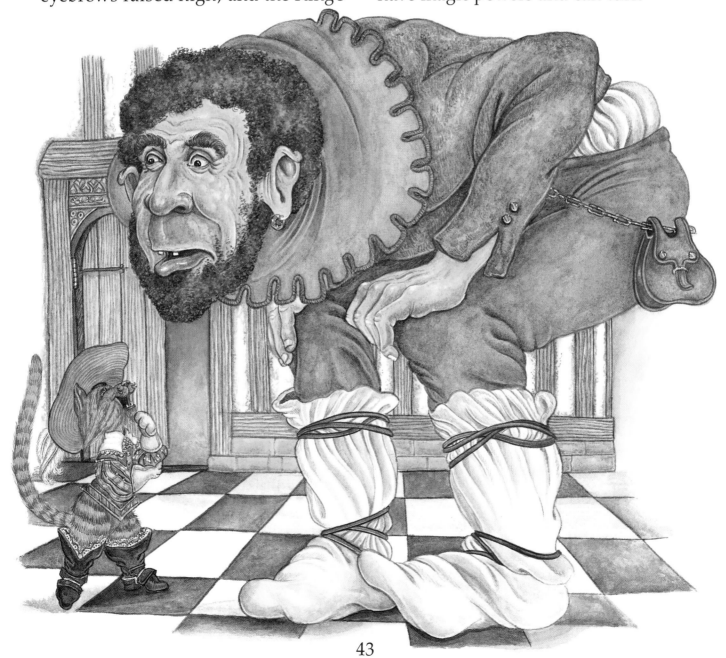

43

yourself into an elephant, but I'm sure they're wrong."

"You are a fool!" shouted the ogre, and turned himself into an elephant, just to prove that he could. The cat shook with terror but said, "Very nice. But the fishermen in the lake said you could turn yourself into a lion. I doubt you can do that."

"Grrr!" roared the ogre, and instantly he was a lion.

"Quite amazing!" said Puss, though he shivered with fright. "But the hunters in the forest said you *couldn't* turn yourself into a mouse, and I believe them."

"I'll show *you*!" shouted the ogre, and became a tiny squeaking mouse. The cat put one paw upon the mouse's tail to keep it from running away, and then scooped up the mouse and gobbled it down.

When the King's carriage went past the ogre's castle, the King asked, "And whose beautiful home might this be?" But Puss was in front of the castle, waving to the carriage and calling, "Welcome to the home of the Marquis of Carabas!"

The King, his daughter, and the poor miller's young son got out of the carriage, and after being dazzled by the elegant castle, the King gave his permission right then and there for his daughter to marry the Marquis of Carabas.

So the King's daughter and the miller's son got married that very night. And Puss himself carried the end of the bride's long train, and never tripped over his own boots, not even once.

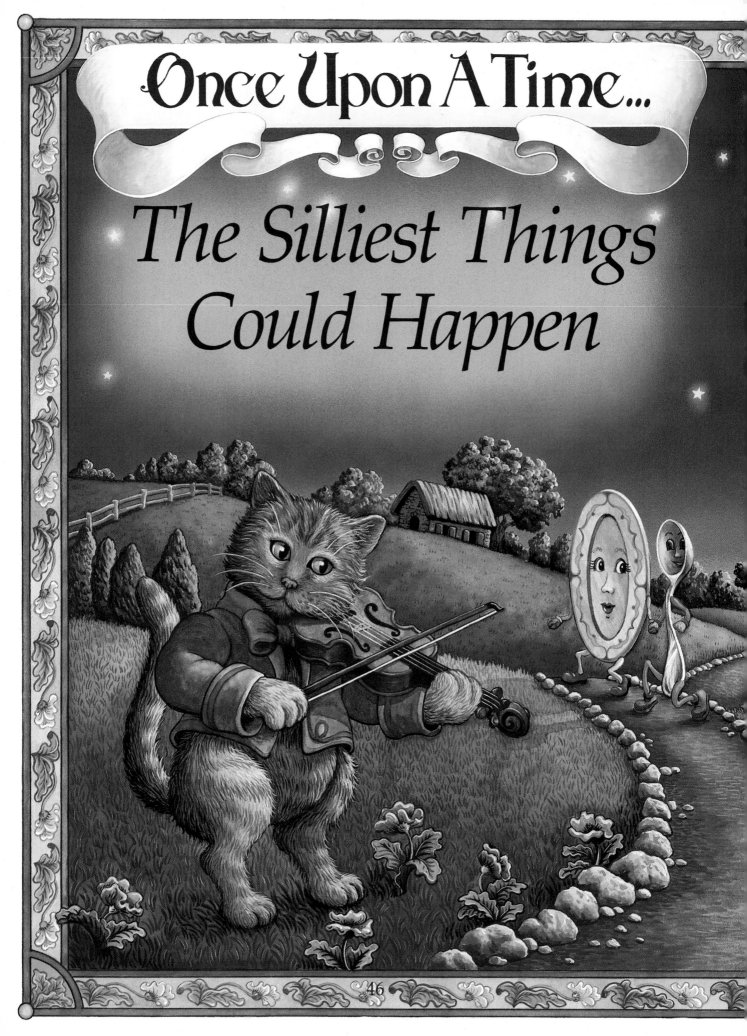

Once Upon A Time...

The Silliest Things Could Happen

Hey, Diddle, Diddle

Hey, diddle, diddle,
The cat and the fiddle,
The cow jumped over the moon;
The little dog laughed
To see such sport,
And the dish ran away with the spoon.

Mother Goose

The Emperor's New Clothes

A Retelling of the Fairy Tale by Hans Christian Andersen

nce upon a time, in a land far away, there lived a rich and powerful emperor who loved nothing better than new clothes. Whenever he did something—whether it was hunting, giving medals to soldiers, or even visiting kings of other lands—it was only to show off his newest outfit. He cared nothing for anything else.

One day, two men appeared at the Emperor's court and announced that they had created the most fashionable cloth ever. The cloth was of the most brilliant colors; the patterns were the most splendid ever seen. The most amazing thing of all about this cloth was that it could be seen only by those who were very smart.

Anyone who was boring or not smart would see nothing at all. The Emperor immediately ordered a suit made of the wonderful cloth, paying the two men lots of money.

The men were given a large room in the palace. Great looms were ordered, as were fine silks and golden thread. Then the two men set to work—*pretending* to weave their fine fabric. They were really weaving nothing at all.

The Emperor wanted to see the new fabric. But he was a bit nervous. After all, he remembered, this was a special fabric — one that only smart people could see. "Of course, *I'll* have no problem seeing it," he thought. "But it might be best if one of the smartest lords from my court were to see it first."

And so a lord was sent to the

workroom to see the wondrous cloth. There were the two men, working away. They spoke of how lovely the fabric was, and how beautiful the colors were. But the lord couldn't see anything.

"Good heavens!" thought the lord. "I must be stupid! I must be an idiot! If the Emperor finds out, he will chop off my head! I must not tell anyone that I cannot see the cloth."

So the terrified lord went to the Emperor and told him that the cloth was the most beautiful he had ever seen.

Time went by, and the Emperor was growing impatient for his new suit, but he still didn't think it a good idea to see the cloth just yet. "Of course, *I'll* see it as soon as I walk into the room!" he thought. "But since it's not finished yet, I'll have my oldest and smartest minister see it first."

And so the oldest and smartest minister went to see the fabric. As the two men told him about the marvelous beauty of the cloth that wasn't really there, he thought to himself, "I can't see anything, yet I'm sure I'm not a fool. But if the Emperor thinks I'm a fool, my head will be chopped off! I must never tell a soul I couldn't see the cloth."

So the minister went back to the Emperor praising the loveliness of the cloth.

Soon the Emperor could wait no longer. He gathered all the lords,

50

ladies, and ministers of the court together and led them to the workroom. There were the two men, working at their empty loom as before. "Isn't this fabric the most beautiful you've ever seen?" they said together.

The Emperor was horrified. He could see nothing! "Am I unfit to be emperor?" he thought. "If anyone finds out, they will take my throne from me! They will run me out of the country! I'm the only one who can't see the fabric! I mustn't let anyone know."

So the Emperor turned to all in the room and said grandly, "Wonderful fabric! Superb!"

And all the lords, ladies, and ministers, thinking themselves idiots for not seeing the fine cloth, also said, "Wonderful! Superb!"

There was to be a great parade the following day, and everyone agreed that the Emperor should lead it dressed in new clothes made from the fine fabric. The two men locked the door to their workroom and burned candles all night so everyone would think they were working hard on the new clothes.

Early the next morning, the Emperor and all the court hurried to the workroom. The two men pretended to hold up each garment. "Beautiful! Delightful!" everyone cried, staring hard but seeing nothing.

The two men then said, "Since you

are pleased, your Majesty, won't you take off those ordinary clothes and put on these new ones?" The Emperor quickly agreed, and the two men pretended they were helping him put on his new finery. All the people of the court praised the clothes, even though the Emperor was wearing nothing but his plain old underwear.

The parade soon began. As the Emperor slowly walked through the streets, all the people cried, "Look at those magnificent clothes! Aren't they lovely?" Nobody dared to admit they couldn't see the new clothes. Nobody wanted their friends or neighbors to think they were fools.

"But he is only wearing old underwear," said a child.

Suddenly everyone began to whisper to each other, "Listen to the child! The Emperor really *isn't* wearing new clothes! The child is right!"

The Emperor knew it was true. But all he could do was hold his head high and continue walking.

MAKE YOUR OWN FAIRY TALE

Make up your own fairy tale!
Point to the picture that you would like to use to finish each sentence.
The story can be as serious or as silly as you like.

nce upon a time there was a

One day she decided to go out and seek a

On the way she met a mean

"Stop!" he said. "I won't let you seek *anything* unless you bring me a

"But how will I ever get it?" asked our heroine. "It is guarded by a fierce

"Too bad!" he said. "If you don't get it for me, I will turn you into a

Our poor heroine had no choice. So off she went. Soon she found herself lost in the

She tried to find her way out, but she just went around in circles. She sat down to cry.
"What's the matter, my dear?" asked a voice above her. It was a little

"I'm lost," said our heroine. "Don't worry," said the

"Just take this magic

and follow the path it shows you."
Our heroine did just that. Soon she found the

 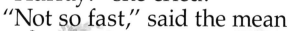 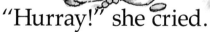 

"Hurray!" she cried.
"Not so fast," said the mean

56

"You didn't bring me what I wanted.
So I won't let you take the

until you kiss me!"
"Never!" she said. And she pulled out the magic

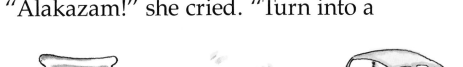

"Alakazam!" she cried. "Turn into a

To her surprise, the magic worked! She went home with her

and lived happily ever after.

The End

57

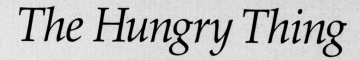

The Hungry Thing

by Jan Slepian and Ann Seidler

ne morning a Hungry Thing came to town. He sat on his tail. He pointed to a sign around his neck that said Feed Me. The townspeople gathered around to see the Hungry Thing.

"What would you like to eat?" asked the townspeople.

"Shmancakes," answered the Hungry Thing.

"Shmancakes!" cried the townspeople. "How do you eat them? What can they be?"

"Why, dear me," said a Wiseman,
"Shmancakes, that's plain,
Are a small kind of chicken that
falls with the rain."

"Of course," said a Cook,
"shmancakes, I've read,
Are better to eat when you stand
on your head."

"I think," said a little boy, "you're
all very silly.
Shmancakes...sound like
Fancakes...sound like...
Pancakes to me."
So the townspeople gave the
Hungry Thing some.

The Hungry Thing ate them all
up. Then the Hungry Thing pointed
to his sign that said Feed Me.

"What would you like to eat?"
asked the townspeople.

"Tickles," answered the Hungry
Thing.

"Tickles!" cried the townspeople. "How do you eat them? What can they be?"

"Why, dear me," said the Wiseman, "tickles, you know,

Are curly tailed hot dogs that grow in a row."

"Of course," said the Cook, "tickles taste yummy,

And you giggle and laugh with ten in your tummy!"

"I think," said the little boy, "it's all very clear.

Tickles . . . sound like

Sickles . . . sound like . . .

Pickles to me."

And they gave the Hungry Thing some.

The Hungry Thing ate them all up. He again pointed to his sign that said Feed Me.

"What would you like to eat this time?" asked the townspeople.

"Hookies," answered the Hungry Thing.

"Hookies!" cried the townspeople. "How do you eat them? What can they be?"

"Hookies," said the Wiseman, "are known in far lands

As a special spaghetti to eat holding hands."

"Hookies," said the Cook, "are a party dish

To serve to a guest if he isn't a fish."

60

"I think," said the little boy, "that it's all very simple.

Hookies...sound like
Lookies...sound like...
Cookies to me."

The townspeople gave the Hungry Thing some. And he ate them all up. Then he got to his feet. He smiled. He patted his mouth on a line of laundry. He turned around three times.

"Is it true
He's all through?"
Asked a lady
Dressed in blue.
"Let's all try
To say goodbye,"
Said a man
With a can.

But the Hungry Thing just sat down again. And he pointed to his sign that said Feed Me.

63

"Oh, please!" said the people.
"We've been here all day.
Isn't there a quicker way?"
"I think," said the boy, "that there is."
"Have some noodles?" the little
boy asked the Hungry Thing. The
Hungry Thing shook his head.
"Oh, excuse me. I meant to say. . .
foodles."
The Hungry Thing smiled and ate
them all up.
"Just look!"
Said the cook.
"Let's all try!
Was the cry.
So they all got busy.
"Have some smello."
They gave him some Jello.
"Have some thread."
They gave him some bread.
"Have a fanana."
They gave him a banana.
The Hungry Thing ate and ate.
He looked very full.

"Is there anything more we can give you?" the townspeople wanted to know.

The Hungry Thing politely covered a hiccup. He thought for a while.

Then . . .

"Boop with a smacker," he said.

"Boop with a smacker? Boop with a smacker? What is that?" the townspeople asked.

The boy whispered to the Wiseman. The Wiseman whispered to the Cook.

And the Cook gave the Hungry Thing . . .

Soup with a cracker.

The Hungry Thing ate them all up. He smiled. He got to his feet. He wiped his mouth on the Cook's hat. Just as he left he turned his sign around.

In big letters it said, THANK YOU!

63

Little People™ Big Book About MAGICAL WORLDS

TIME-LIFE for CHILDREN™

Publisher: Robert H. Smith
Managing Director: Neil Kagan
Editorial Directors: Jean Burke Crawford,
　　　　　Patricia Daniels
Editorial Coordinator: Elizabeth Ward
Marketing Director: Ruth P. Stevens
Product Manager: Margaret Mooney
Production Manager: Prudence G. Harris
Administrative Assistant: Rebecca C. Christoffersen
Editorial Consultants: Jacqueline A. Ball,
　　　　　Sara Mark

PRODUCED BY PARACHUTE PRESS, INC.

Editorial Director: Joan Waricha
Editors: Christopher Medina, Jane Stine, Wendy Wax
Writers: Laura Backes, Emily James, Gregory
　　　Maguire, Christopher Medina, Jean
　　　Waricha, Wendy Wax
Designer: Lillian Lovitt
Illustrators: Robert Alley (pp. 12–13, 54–57); L. Nathan
　　　Butler (pp. 36–39); Pat and Robin DeWitt
　　　(pp. 22–25, 40–45); Dennis Hockerman
　　　(pp. 6–11, 20–21, 26–27); Allan Neuwirth
　　　(pp. 58–63); John O'Brien (pp. 48–53); Carol
　　　Schwartz (pp. 4–5, 28–29, 46–47); Gill Speirs
　　　(endpapers); John Speirs (cover, pp. 14–19,
　　　30–35).

Time-Life Books Inc. is a wholly owned subsidiary
of THE TIME INC. BOOK COMPANY.

TIME-LIFE is a trademark of Time Warner Inc.
U.S.A.

FISHER-PRICE, LITTLE PEOPLE and AWNING
DESIGN are trademarks of Fisher-Price, Division
of The Quaker Oats Company, and are used under
license.

Time-Life Books Inc. offers a wide range of fine
publications, including home video products. For
subscription information, call 1-800-621-7026 or
write TIME-LIFE BOOKS, P.O. Box C-32068,
Richmond, Virginia 23261-2068.

ACKNOWLEDGMENTS

Every effort has been made to trace the ownership of all copyrighted material and to secure the necessary
permissions to reprint these selections. If any question arises as to the use of any material, the editor and the
publisher, while expressing regret for any inadvertent error, will make the necessary correction in future
printings.

Grateful acknowledgment is made to the following for permission to reprint copyrighted material: Farrar,
Straus & Giroux for "Unicorn" from LAUGHING TIME by William Jay Smith. Copyright © 1955, 1957, 1980,
1990 by William Jay Smith. Harper & Row Publishers, Inc. for "This Bridge" from A LIGHT IN THE ATTIC by
Shel Silverstein. Copyright © 1981 by Evil Eye Music, Inc. Scholastic Book Services for THE HUNGRY THING
by Jan Slepian and Ann Seidler. Copyright © 1967 by Janice B. Slepian and Ann G. Seidler.

Library of Congress Cataloging-in-Publication Data

Little people big book about magical worlds.
　　Summary: A collection of fairy tales, nursery rhymes, and related activities and games.
　　ISBN 0-8094-7495-6—ISBN 0-8094-7496-4 (lib. bdg.)
　　1. Fairy tales. 2. Tales. [1. Fairy tales. 2. Folklore] I. Time-Life for Children (Firm) II. Title: About magical worlds.
PZ8.L7197 1990　　　　　　　　　　　398.21 [E]　　　　　　　　　　　90-11040

TIME-LIFE BOOKS
ALEXANDRIA, VIRGINIA

This Bridge

This bridge will only take you halfway there
To those mysterious lands you long to see:
Through gypsy camps and swirling Arab fairs
And moonlit woods where unicorns run free.
So come and walk awhile with me and share
The twisting trails and wondrous worlds I've known.
But this bridge will only take you halfway there —
The last few steps you'll have to take alone.

Shel Silverstein